WHY THERE ARE WAVES ON THE SEA

Written by Eric Pullin

Illustrated by Chris Davis

(Student at Stevenson College Edinburgh)

WHY THERE ARE WAVES ON THE SEA
copyright 2007 Eric Pullin

ISBN No: 978-1-903172-96-4
First published by Barny Books 2007

Publishers: Barny Books, Hough on the Hill
               Grantham, Lincolnshire, NG32 2BB
  Tel: 01400 250246   www.barnybooks.biz

Printed by Minuteman Press, Edinburgh, Scotland
Tel: 0131 444 0800

Dear Reader,   -

MR BARNY OWL FROM OUR FIRST STORY HAS GOT LOST

> Although I've hunted everywhere
> I can't find Owl – he isn't there.
> He must be hiding in this book
> So please be kind and take a look
> And if you spot him write to me
> I might just send you something FREE

Where's Barny? Write to eric.pullin@tiscali.co.uk and tell me.

Visit our website at www.thewhyseries.co.uk

Wilberforce the baby whale
Was proud of his enormous tail.
His brothers and his sisters said
He'd let his tail go to his head.
They called him names then off they'd swim
They didn't want to play with him.

So Wilberforce would spend his day
Just looking for new friends to play.
When shoals of fish came swimming by
The little whale would shout out, "Hi,
I'm Wilberforce the baby whale
Just look at my fantastic tail."

The other fish just turned their heads
And swam off to their coral beds.
They didn't seem to care at all
If Wilbur's tail was big or small.
Alone again, the baby whale
Was left to chase his favourite tail.

9

For Wilberforce the deep blue sea
Was such a lonely place to be
And soon he found it hard to hide
The sadness that he felt inside.
It's no use trying to pretend
Life's fun - without a single friend.

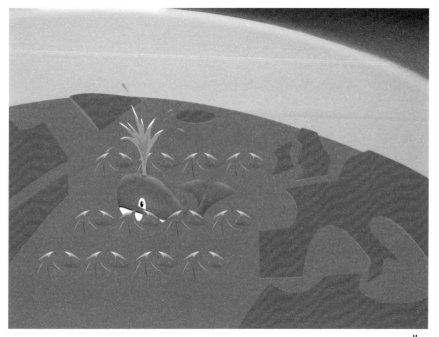

When Wilbur's mother asked one day,

"Why aren't you going off to play?"

The tears that he'd been trying to hide

Began to gush from Wilbur's eyes.

Between the sobs the baby whale

Cried, "Please give me a smaller tail."

13

And, bit-by-bit, he told his Mum
How sad and lonely he'd become
And how his tail just seemed to be
The cause of all his misery.
"I'm so ashamed," poor Wilbur said,
"I let my tail go to my head."

"Just you leave everything to me,"
Said Wilbur's Mum, "you wait and see.
Dry those tears and try to smile.
I'll be back in a little while."
She kissed his cheek - then off she swam
To set about her special plan.

Wilbur's mother swam around
And every creature that she found
She asked if they would like to play
A special game - on Saturday.
"The sunken wreck is where we'll be
And don't be late - it starts at 3!"

That night his mum told Wilbur's dad

Of how their son was very sad.

She told him what she planned to do,

"I'm going to need some help from you."

And Wilbur's dad soon understood

And off he swam to find some wood.

The special day soon came around.

Sea creatures flocked from miles around

And as they reached the wreck - their eyes

Popped out with wonder and surprise.

Floating on the sea they saw

A sight they'd never seen before.

23

Made from wood to make them float
Were dozens of the strangest boats.
"Not boats," said Mr Whale, "These craft
Are what us old sea dogs call rafts.
So climb on board - then I'll explain
The rules of our new racing game."

25

Mr Whale just watched and laughed
As every brightly coloured craft
Was filled with creatures big and small,
"No need to push – There's room for all."
When everyone had found a place
Mr Whale explained the race.

27

"Because these rafts have got no sails
When I say "GO" the baby whales
Will splash their tails with all their might
So, please make sure you hang on tight.
The waves they make, I think you'll find,
Will drive you to the winning line."

FINISH

29

And then the baby whales appeared
And everybody stood and cheered.
Each wore a football strip that matched
The colour of their own team's craft.
They thrashed and splashed their mighty tails
And on the waves the racers sailed.

The biggest waves were made, of course,

By someone known as Wilberforce.

His Red team won the race that day

And now his friends just love to play

When Wilberforce the baby whale,

Makes waves with his enormous tail.

So now, when you're beside the sea

And wondering why it should be

That waves are lapping on the sand

You'll think of whales and understand

That, somewhere, in a far off place,

They're practising for their next race.

35

Author's note

Writing "The Why Series" is easy. The difficult part is getting the stories from inside my head to in front of your eyes and there are many people that I would like to thank for the help that they have given me in doing this.

Chris, my brilliant illustrator. Jayne and Molly at my publishers, Barny Books. Richard and the staff at Minuteman Press, my printers. Marjory and Ronnie and the students at Stevenson College Edinburgh. Special thanks to my wife Penny and my sister Gill together with the rest of my family for their constant encouragement and support.

Last but not least my beautiful grand daughters Lucy and Lulah for whom these stories were originally written.
I am indebted to you all.

www.thewhyseries.co.uk